Queen of the Sea

DYLAN MECONIS

WALKER
BOOKS

1

7

8

I wasn't born on
the Island.

If you're reading this to find out what
happened to the true queen of Albion,
that's the first thing you should know.

Trust me.

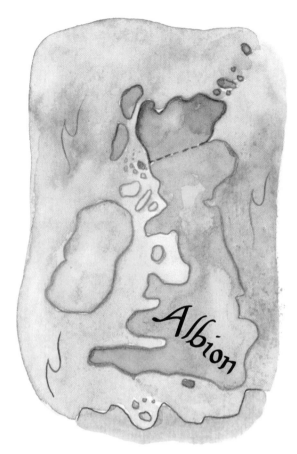

The funny thing is,

I don't know where I was born.

It might have been on a much, much bigger island, not too far away, called *Albion*.

Albion is also the name of the kingdom our little Island belongs to.

There are many other islands included in the kingdom of Albion, of all sizes and shapes.

In fact, the whole kingdom is nothing but islands. I suppose that I could have been born on any of them!

I don't even know the exact day I was born— only that it was almost twelve years ago.

We celebrate my birth on Saint Elysia's Day instead. That's the day I was brought to the Island aboard a ship called the *Regina Maris*.

I can't remember that day at all. I was only a baby.

But I do know exactly what happened, down to the last detail. How?

Well, starting on the morning of my sixth Saint Elysia's Day on the Island,

I decided to ask every single person on the Island about it.

That may sound like a lot of work for a very small girl.

I II III IV V VI VII VIII IX X

But since there were only ten other people on the Island, it didn't take very long at all.

And since the Regina Maris is the only ship that comes to the Island, and since it only visits twice a year...

Spring

and Autumn

...absolutely everybody was there to see me arrive.

My name is **Margaret**, by the way.

Not "Lady Margaret of Somewhere" or "Sister Margaret" or even "Mistress Margaret So-and-So." Just Margaret.

Margaret means **pearl**, which makes it a good name for me. Pearls are hidden inside oysters, deep beneath the waves, and our Island is hidden far from the rest of Albion, deep into the Silver Sea. Our Island is so small, and so far away, that it doesn't have a proper name. It isn't even on some maps!

The only reason that anybody lives there at all is the **convent**. A convent is a place where women go to lead very religious lives together without ordinary people around to distract them.

A woman who makes a promise to live forever in a convent becomes a nun and calls herself a sister. After you become a nun you aren't allowed to get married or have any children.

Being a nun is not very easy, but there are plenty of reasons to become one, especially if you like to help people. Different orders help different people.

Some Kinds of Nuns (But There Are Others!)

Clarites
Nurse
the sick

Wandering
Sisters
Shelter travelers

Lamentines
Pray for
prisoners

Elysians
That's us!

The convent on the Island belongs to the *Elysian order*.

Elysian nuns live by the sea and honor *Saint Elysia* by taking care of sailors and their families.

Our part of the Silver Sea is full of storms and tricky currents.

The convent was built here so that Elysian sisters could pray for the safety of all the ships that go by and take care of anybody who washes up on the Island after a shipwreck.

Those are important jobs, but nowadays the sisters don't have to do them very often. Not many ships sail by anymore.

In the past, every time Albion declared war on its enemy kingdom, *Gallia*...

or Gallia declared war on Albion,

or everybody just decided it was time for another war,

it became much more dangerous for ships to sail through the *Silken Sleeve*, the bit of water between Albion and Gallia.

Instead, they sailed the long way around—past our Island.

the Island

Albion

the Silken Sleeve

Gallia

Then our king, Edmund, ended the wars for good. He defeated Gallia so badly that they declared a truce. So now nobody needs to take the long, dangerous route past us.

The only sailors who the sisters of the Island have to pray for these days are the ones who belong to the *Regina Maris*. And the only person who washed up on the Island needing their care and attention...was me.

What had happened on that day?

Sisters

Sister Barbara...is the **Sacrist**.
She makes sure we have enough candles and incense, and cleans and decorates the church.

We said special prayers for you that night.

Poor little lamb!

Ha!

Sister Wynefreed

...is the **Cellarer**. It's her job to see that we have enough food in the gardens and cellar.

You may have looked like a lamb...

but you squealed like a piglet!

Buk.

and...

Sister Philippa

...takes care of all the animals in our farmyard.

Next, I asked... the Servants

Maud is the **Kitchener**, which means she's in charge of...yes, the kitchen.

Her husband was a ship's captain. Elysian nuns saved his life once.

After he died, Maud took their daughters and came to work on the Island.

> I fed you sweet milk porridge,
>
> though you looked too small even to be weaned.

> I put an iron horseshoe over the door,
>
> so the fairies wouldn't steal you and replace you with an imp.

> You wouldn't stop crying...
>
> until I put you to sleep between us in the bed.

Bess is Maud's older daughter. She mostly helps with cooking.

Tess is Maud's younger daughter. She mostly helps with cleaning.

Last of all, I tried to ask...

Father Ambrose

Nuns are generally very holy people. But there are some important things that only a priest can do, and only men are allowed to become priests.

In a normal convent, a priest would visit once in a while to take care of all those things and then travel on to other convents and leave the sisters in peace. But since we're so far away from other convents, Father Ambrose just stays put.

Father Ambrose is **very good** at staying put.

I doubt you would learn much from him, Margaret.

He's lost his memory.

Where did it go?

Nowhere that you could find, moppet.

I didn't learn much from the other residents of the Island, either.

Because they're all... # Animals

Hugh, the dog, herds the other
animals and keeps them out
of trouble. He also cleans
the kitchen floor.

Sebastian is the cat. Don't let his
handsome looks fool you. He is very
cruel to the mice he catches.

Walter is the horse. He helps
carry heavy things across the Island.
He is very fond of apples.

The billy goat
is
Henry
and the
nanny goats
are
Lettice, Rosie,
and Ethel.

There are plenty of hens, but they never have names.

We eat the birds that aren't very good at laying eggs, and it seems cruel to roast something named Marcella or Elizabeth.

There is only ever one rooster at a time, and he is always named Padraigh. (I don't know why.)

ROOo -a- ROO-a- ROoooooooooooooooOOO

The bees that give us wax and honey are too many to count, so I call them all Beatrice.

Very funny.

Tess thought of a way I might be able to learn something from the animals—

According to legend...

animals can speak at Midwinter midnight!

But Midwinter was far off, and sneaking out of bed wouldn't exactly be easy, anyway.

SNoRrr

So that was the end of my asking questions.

What have you learned, Margaret?

That I was very small. That it was a Friday. That it rained.

That I had porridge.

That I cried until I went to bed.

That is a great deal to know about a single day.

Yes.

Did you learn all that you hoped to?

Sister Agnes...

why did I come to the Island?

I cannot say,

though I am very glad you are here.

24

I was very glad that I lived on the Island.

And, after all, I couldn't really miss a mother or father I had never known...could I?

Still, I was envious of the children I knew who did have parents.
There were two children like that on the Island, and I saw them every day.

They just weren't **real** children.

This is the statue of...

the Mournful Mother.

She protects the Island
and everybody on it, and all
the sailors on the Silver Sea,
and Albion that sits in it, and
even Gallia and the rest of
the Continent, and the whole
world beyond that.

She shows mercy to anyone
who needs it, and she is never
tired from all this work.

In her arms
is her child,

the Sorrowful Son.

They live in the church.
They are made of wood.

28

The other "child" on the Island was in a painting hung in the **Chapter House**, which is the big room where everybody gathers for important meetings or special announcements.

It was a picture of

King Edmund,

the ruler of Albion, with his daughter Eleanor.

At first, because of her red hair, I thought that the little girl in the picture might be *me*.

(Although her ball was much fancier than my wooden one.)

No, dear. That's the **crown princess.**

What does that mean, Sister Sybil?

It means she is the king's daughter and that she will rule the kingdom after him. Unless he has a son.

I found out later that she wasn't even holding a ball to play with but an important thing called a *globus cruciger* that represents the whole world and means you are a person who rules over part of it. (With God's permission, of course.)

So I wasn't jealous of her useless ball anymore. But she did have a father who let her sit on his lap. I thought that he must be very proud of her and love her very much.

Sometimes I would visit the painting of the princess
and her father the king and imagine for a little while
that it really was me sitting on his lap, and that he told
me stories of the wicked world and all the ways a good
and kind ruler could make it better.

Or I would visit the statue of the Mournful Mother
and pretend that I had once been a baby made of
wood on her lap, and that She had brought me to life
and given me to the sisters of the Island so that one
of her children wouldn't grow up to be so sad.

No one could be sad living on the Island, I thought. But since my living there
meant that I couldn't have my real mother and father with me, I decided that
it was reasonable to ask God for something in return.

The one thing
I really wanted...

30

That is how I met William.

In the first six years I had lived on the Island,

nobody new had come to stay. (Well, other than chickens.)

Every time the *Regina Maris* appeared in the bay, Captain Marley would row ashore on the longboat with some of his sailors to unload all our supplies for the next half-year.

Next, Captain Marley would share a meal with Sister Agnes, tell her all the news from Albion, and exchange all the letters and packages they had to send or to deliver.

Then all the sailors would row back to the ship before dark,

and they would be gone by the morning.

(After all, it's not very proper for a bunch of sailors to spend the night at a convent.)

So, the next time that the *Regina Maris* arrived in the bay, I could tell right away that something was different.

For one thing,

sailors don't wear fine cloaks.

35

But William's mother, Lady Cameron, didn't fit in so well, not even after three years. Some days she never left her bed. She hardly ever helped the sisters with their embroidery, which paid for all the food we could not grow ourselves. I thought she was very selfish.

Lady Cameron, we have wool and dye enough left over, if you'd care for a gown in a new color.

No. It's black I will wear until the end of my days, for my husband and my father are gone from me.

My husband died of fever when I was half your age, Lady Cameron.

I find **blue** wears the loss just as well.

I thought the sisters had all grown up as foundlings, like me, or had taken vows because they wanted to serve Saint Elysia instead of being married. Sister Wynefreed had not only had a husband, but lost him! Yet she had found peace in the sisterhood. So why did Lady Cameron not take her vows and find peace, too?

Maybe it had something to do with how her husband had died.

My father died in glorious battle, as a lord of the blood should.

Who was he in battle with?

The king.

The king of where?

The king of Albion, of course. King Edmund.

But that's our king.

He hasn't always been, and he won't always be, either. Not of *Ecossia*, anyway!

My mother says that after the battle, my brothers and uncles rode north to the rebel territories of Old Ecossia,

and as soon as they have men enough they will avenge my father and take back our lands,

and I shall join them, and my mother will live in our Castle Cameron again,

and we will be happy.

I was confused because a good king wouldn't take anybody's home away, and King Edmund was a good king. And because I thought that William was already happy. Who needed anything more than what was on the Island? We explored every inch of it together.

the Kitchen Garden

Sister Wynefreed grows turnips, beets, parsnips, onions, garlic, and radishes.

My favorite is radishes. My least favorite is turnips. Guess which one she plants much, much more of.

the Orchard

We grow apples and pears to turn into jam and ciders.

the Stone Circle

the Quarry Pond

All the stones in the convent buildings were dug out of this quarry centuries ago. It's been filling up with rainwater ever since, and now it's a pond! Good for swimming in.

the
Graveyard
This is where sailors who died on
the Island after storms or wrecks
are buried. I don't believe in ghosts.

the
Barrow

the
Homeward
Cliffs

the
Stairway

the
Beach

to Albion

the
Seal Rock

the
Goat Hills
Our goats and their kids like to jump
around on all the rocks and lumps here.
Watch out for droppings!!!

Some parts of the Island were more unusual
or interesting than others. For example,
in the east part of the Island are...

the Homeward Cliffs.

The Island has cliffs all around it, but these are the highest by far. The wind on
this part of the Island is so strong that hardly anything can grow. It faces Albion,
but the only thing you'll see here is the sea, the sea, the sea.

If the wind was blowing from the west, William and I would let go of
leaves or feathers to see whose was carried away farther or fastest.

On the north side of the church is a strangely shaped hill called... the Barrow.

43

The Barrow isn't the only sign that the Old People left behind. In the middle of the Island is a ring of carefully balanced rocks called...

the Stone Circle

What is it for?

Most likely to tell the time of year, from how the shadows were cast.

But how could they know that it would work?

People knew many things even then.

But they didn't know about the Sorrowful Son. So they were heathens!

There are many kinds of useful knowledge that came from the ancients, Margaret—

like how to navigate a ship by looking at the stars.

There's only one place on the Island where you can get down to the sea (well, without jumping).

The Stairway is a path that goes down through the cliffside that leads to the beach.

Sister Sybil taught us that the Stairway probably began when an ancient stream carved a groove into the cliffside.

Eventually the stream went dry, and the Old People used its old bed as a pathway to climb up and down between the top of the Island and the Beach.

Then, hundreds of years later, the same people who built the convent carved the rock into an actual staircase to make it even easier to bring things up from the beach. It's still steep, but not so bad unless you're carrying something heavy.

(Unfortunately, the driftwood that we bring up from the beach to dry out and burn as fuel is very heavy!)

So many feet have gone up and down the stairs that the middle part of every step is worn down. Someday the Stairway may turn **back** into a streambed!

The noise of the waves is very strange in the Stairway. It sounds small and far away, but loud at the same time, like the sound of Sister Philippa's beehives.

Sometimes when the wind blows straight into the Stairway, it feels like it's trying to suck away your breath.

The Beach is worth the long trip down. At low tide, it looks like this:

And at high tide, it looks like this. In the winter the waves are so high and so angry that even at low tide there's hardly any beach at all.

In the summertime, the low tide can go out so far that more than half of the dock is on dry land, and all the creatures who live near the tide line go thirsty for a few hours.

Ahhh...

Fie!

The convent has a little fishing boat
that you can launch from the dock.
It's a coracle, which is a sort of basket
boat woven out of strips of wood and grass.

You couldn't sail anywhere with it,
but it's easy to row out into the bay,
where the tastiest fish live.

Fishing does get a little dull. You cast
your nets or put out your lines and
then there isn't much else to do.

The water is usually too cold to swim in—
although that doesn't mean it hasn't happened!

It's a good thing that Sister Philippa had already taught us how to swim.

I'm under here.

I just...wanted to get it back for you.

Don't tell my mother this happened.

But Lady Cameron did find out about it, from Sister Philippa. Nuns aren't allowed to lie. Lady Cameron told Sister Agnes that William couldn't go out in the coracle anymore, and that he and I weren't allowed to see each other for—

An entire month?

That's not fair! It was just an accident!

Fishing became very boring again.

Thankfully, Sister Philippa became too busy with the farm, so Tess took me instead. As the fish moved into the cooler water of the bay, we drifted close enough for me to spy on the inhabitants of—

the Seal Rock

All the seals in the nearby sea gather there to sun themselves, sleep with their pups, or gossip between fish hunts.

Look—there's a white seal!

That one is a selkie for sure.

Maybe even the Queen of the Sea!

What's a selkie?

A selkie is a magical seal-maiden.

She wears a sealskin and lives among her people in the sea.

But if she doesn't find a husband among seals, she may take off her sealskin and fall in love with a human fisherman!

She may marry him, and even have children with him, and as long as he keeps her sealskin locked away, they can live happily for years.

But someday,

the sea will call her home.

When the long month was over, and Lady Cameron finally let William come outside with me again, I told him all about the white seal and the legend of the selkie.

A few months later, the Island was struck by an enormous storm.

KLANG KLANG KLA

He won't come!

Convince him quickly, before he's blown out to sea!

57

Elysia had no brothers or sisters and she hadn't married anybody yet.

Her father sailed ships full of valuable spices to faraway ports.

He would be gone for months at a time.

Elysia stayed home because the sea is a dangerous place, especially for a maiden.

One day news came that her father's ship had been sunk by Rolf the Pirate King

and her father had drowned.

Elysia was left alone and with no means of support.

Luckily, Elysia wasn't the sort of person to give up.

She decided to run her father's business herself.

Some of the sailors thought she was

crazy!

Elysia didn't care. She sailed across the sea five times without any trouble. But on her sixth voyage, her ship was captured...

by Rolf the Pirate King

This one is Rolf.

regular pirate

other regular pirate

But even pirates couldn't frighten Elysia.

Elysia was very faithful and always said her prayers. Before long she had converted the whole crew and convinced them to give up piracy!

Rolf the Pirate King was **NOT** happy about this.

He thought Elysia was a *witch* and that she had cast a spell on his crew.

That was bad, but he decided that having a witch around could be pretty useful in the pirate business.

So he told Elysia,

Marry me! ...or else!

But Elysia said,

NO

Which was very brave,
but since she said her prayers
so often, Elysia knew it was
the right thing to do.

So Rolf threw her overboard.

I warned you!

Elysia sank and sank. (She didn't know how to swim.)

She thought she would probably drown.

But she wasn't scared.

When you've done the right thing, dying doesn't seem so bad. Elysia knew she would go to heaven.

So she said her prayers all the way to the bottom of the sea.

The fish heard her praying!

Then something **amazing** happened.

All the fish in the sea rose up and carried Elysia to the surface. Then they told her to stand on their backs, and they took her all the way home to Albion.

It was a miracle!

Elysia was so grateful for her miracle that as soon as she got home, she decided to take up the holy life and become a nun.

She sold her father's business and gave all the money to the widows and daughters of sailors lost at sea.

Many of them decided they wanted to become nuns, too. So Elysia founded her very own order!

Elysian sisters live in convents by the shore or on islands, like ours.

And Saint Elysia is the patron saint of anybody whose life or love is at the mercy of the sea.

The End

(nuns)

(more nuns)

(not actually this small)

The next morning we all went outside to see what other damage the storm had done. Normally the sisters are silent for most of the day, but Sister Agnes lifted the vow so everybody could discuss the repairs. The roof of the church had lost plenty of tiles, and two of the apple trees had been torn up. A window in the Guest House was broken. The kitchen had lost its chimney pot. The chicken house was leaning to the side.

Was this a sin? We hadn't been told not to climb the wall. We hadn't been told not to look over it.

But something about it felt secret, and dangerous.

On the other hand, if William went into the cave alone and was hurt, it would be my fault, and Lady Cameron might punish us both by taking William away again.

71

73

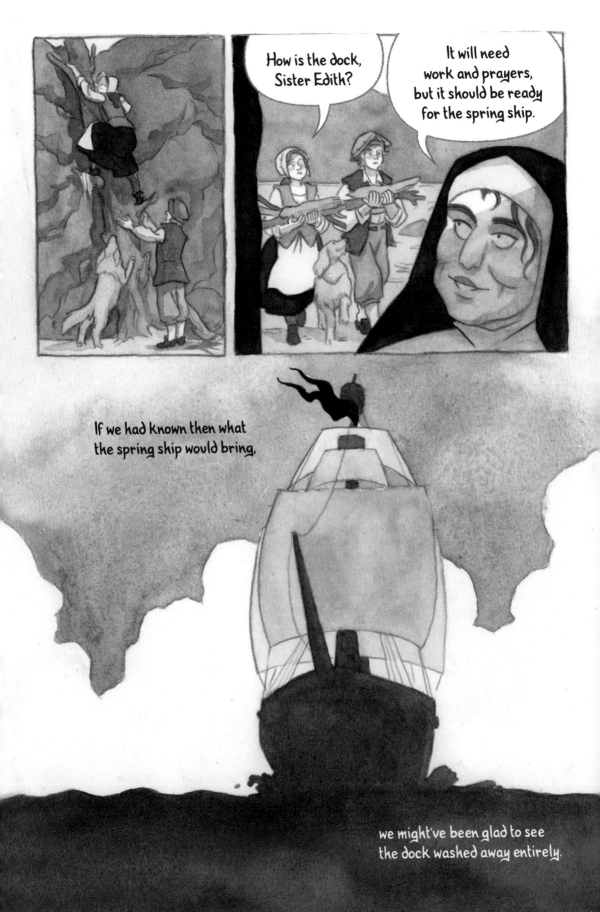

The storm had rearranged **many** things on the Island. The sisters had to set aside most of their usual work to fix it all. Sister Sybil left William and me to do our lessons on our own while she helped Sister Barbara make repairs to the church roof.

That it may...
p...please...thee
to...forg...forg...

Forgive.

The letters are always trading places and turning themselves on their heads. I wish I never had to read from a book again for the rest of my life.

Don't worry. I'll be there to read them for you!

The biggest change the storm brought, though, was to Lady Cameron.

Perhaps I could help, too.

From then on, Lady Cameron sat with William every day to help him with his reading—even after Sister Sybil resumed our usual lessons.

For-give.

Forgive.

She made me recite Saint Elysia's tale to her every day, and she began to visit her chapel in the church as well.

She reminds me that suffering may lead to blessings, too,

if we are ready to accept them.

Storm repairs had set the sisters behind in their embroidery, and she offered to help.

These pieces will never be ready in time.

You must assist me, Margaret.

I don't know how to. Sister Sybil hasn't had time to teach me yet.

Then you shall learn with me. You must know how to do it, if you wish to become a nun.

Embroidery **seems** easy. You put the cloth in a frame to hold it tight, then you put thread on the needle, and then you sew it onto the cloth until it makes a picture. But there's much more to it than that! First you need the supplies.

A canvas panel.
This is just a square of linen that Sister Barbara makes on her loom. For very fancy work, you need silk, which comes on the *Regina Maris*.

Silk thread, called *floss*.

Dyes, if you want to change any colors.

If you want the floss to be gold or silver, you'll need real gold or silver wire, very fine.

You wrap the wire around and around and around the floss, until it's covered.

And, of course, needles, needles, **needles!**

bone

wood

metal

(And a **thimble** to protect your finger from them.)

77

As if that isn't enough to keep track of, there are many different kinds of stitches that are used for specific parts of a picture—to make simple lines or fancy knots or smooth, padded bits.

Appliqué.

Back-stitch.

Split.

Satin.

Knots.

Long and short.

Stem.

Chain.

Couching.

And don't forget the decorative **beads**!

At first, I didn't like embroidery any more than I liked Lady Cameron.

The sisters have asked us to invent a pattern for the edge of their new embroidery of Saint Elysia.

William, you can read to us while we work.

I gradually realized there were a few good things about embroidery and Lady Cameron.

All winter we worked like this together, the three of us. William read us a whole book, while Lady Cameron and I embroidered all the fish in the sea.

It was very
fine, indeed.

And then, all of a sudden, it was spring.
Warm enough to have our lessons by
open windows instead of the hearth.

What about this one?

That book is in Hellenic. It uses a different alphabet.

There's more than one alphabet?!

The Regina Maris! It's come!

But look. It has a black flag. What does that mean?

It means that someone has died.

Sister Sybil left us with Lady Cameron to finish our lessons. An hour went by.

Does it mean somebody on the ship has died?

No. That flag is only flown for important people.

(Were the officers and crew of the *Regina Maris* not important?)

Maybe it's the king!

William! Not so loud!

No. He's too big and strong to just die.

The longboat's landed already— there's Captain Marley!

As well as many of the most important officers of the kingdom,

and hundreds of innocent people in the cities and countryside.

Ah!

It is God's mercy that the princess was spared, or we would have civil war again.

We may have war again anyway.

Will you help, Lady Cameron? This young man is the captain's adopted son. He has a wife and child of his own.

...I will.

William and I were sent down to the kitchen to help Maud and Tess and Bess with the food delivered by the *Regina Maris*. It was even more work than usual because all the sisters except for Sister Edith were saying special prayers for the soul of the king.

What would little Princess Eleanor do without her father's lap to sit in?

86

87

In the morning we crept out of the bedchamber to the kitchen so Lady Cameron could sleep.

92

Sister Agnes wouldn't let us back into the infirmary, or into our bedchamber.
She and Sister Philippa would care for Lady Cameron and Sister Edith on their own.

If we were too young to help the sick, we were old enough to help with everything else.
We did every chore we could on the farm. We did every chore we could in the kitchen.
We even swept the church; we found a nest of mice and let them all go without giving
them to the cat, because Jess told us it was bad luck when somebody nearby was sick.

William.

97

Swear to me that someday you will be free again, William!

And that you will have revenge against our enemies who did this to us!

I do!

...Now take him away! Take him away from here!

Lady Cameron died that evening.

Sister Philippa rang the bell three times.

That is how many times a church bell rings when a lady dies.

All the Island, and Captain Marley, said Mass for her passing that Sunday, so that all our prayers would help lift her soul to heaven.

Sister Edith and Richard Marley were there, for they were mostly well again.

Lady Cameron's body was buried in the crypt beneath the church. I had never seen inside before. It was small, and dark, but there was nothing to be afraid of, for everyone who had been buried there had led a good life.

Even Tess said there were no ghosts at all.

Our old bedchamber was closed up. William slept in a chamber with Captain Marley and Richard, and I slept with Tess and Bess again.

We did not have our lessons. William had no chores. I hardly saw him at all, in fact, and when I did, he barely spoke.

And so I could not ask what he thought about the things Lady Cameron had said to him. Fevers can make people say very strange things.

Finally the Regina Maris was ready to sail.

William! Where are you going?

I am going to the ship.

You mean the longboat?

No. The Regina Maris.

They will take me to Albion, and then I will go to the prison where my brothers and uncles are held.

It is called Highwall Keep. They were never in Old Ecossia.

My mother only told me that so I might have hope for the future,

and not guess that we were prisoners, too.

But why would you have to join them?

Sister Agnes says I am not allowed to stay here without my mother.

That can't be true! This is your home!

She says I am made to go, by law. But since I am a MacCormick and a lord of Cameron, it is good that I go, for I am too old to live among women.

My brothers and uncles will teach me how to be a man, so I will be ready to avenge our family.

Seeking revenge is a sin. You're supposed to forgive your enemies.

Don't you remember everything you read to us this year?

It is a convent, and we are here to serve Saint Elysia.

But the convent, and the Island, have been other things at other times.

After the last war, King Edmund gave this place a second purpose.

That is the safekeeping of women who have angered or hurt the king, or whose families have.

But the sisters. And the servants. And me.

We aren't prisoners. Only Lady Cameron was.

Lady Cameron was kept here by royal order, yes.

When her husband was executed and his kinsmen were taken prisoner, she was allowed to keep William with her, until he came of age.

The servants, and Father Ambrose, are here by choice, to serve the order.

So they were taking William away to another prison, where I would never see him again. Perhaps one with bars over the windows, locks on the doors, and guards at the gates.

We had none of those things here. But only because the Island itself was a prison cell,

and the sea was its walls.

Everyone I loved,
every place on the Island
I cared for, every answer
I had ever gotten to every
question I had ever asked—

was a part of one
huge and terrible lie.

The sisters had not been called in
their souls to follow Saint Elysia;

they had been caught
in a net, like fish.

I was not sent here to be
kept safe. I was kept here
to make somebody else safe.

Kept here by the king.
The wise and good ruler
and the loving father,
who sent a *baby* to prison.

There was only one place
on the Island I could stand
thinking about.

The one place that couldn't
be part of the prison,

because nobody
knew it was there.

The people who had lived there, long ago, were able to leave the Island at any time, in their little boats.

They had found the Island and they had chosen to make it their home, and nobody could order them to stay or to go. Their lives must have been exactly like the pictures on the wall—

rough and simple and secret and true.

I'm going to be one of you instead.

As the hours passed, I listened to the tide roar up and start to fill in the mouth of the cave. I should have been frightened that the tide might go too high and I'd have to swim out, or that I'd be drowned or washed out to sea.

Or that the tide would bring in flotsam and block the cave and I'd be trapped.

Or that a sea monster would swim up through the cave and eat me whole.

But I wasn't afraid of any of those things.

It was the first night in my life that I was free.

Nothing happened to me that night in the cave.

I didn't even dream.

In the morning, when the tide had gone out again, I went back to the convent. I was soaked in seawater and dirty, but nobody asked where I had been.

Sister Agnes wasn't angry, even though everybody had been looking for me.

How could she be angry that I had done one bad thing, when I was already a prisoner, despite having done no bad things at all? What could she do to me?

Shut me away alone in my bedchamber? I slept alone now, anyway.

Smack my hand with a wooden spoon for being naughty? I was too old for that.

Send me to Highwall Keep, to live with William? I almost hoped she would.

In the end, she made me apologize to the sisters who went looking for me, and say extra prayers, and do extra chores, and read a long, boring book.

That was all.

She didn't even raise her voice. Nuns aren't supposed to be angry.

But I wasn't a nun.

The days grew longer and the nights grew shorter.

The rooster was let in with one of the hens and there were new chicks, but I didn't visit them.

I embroidered a perfect rose. Lady Cameron would have been proud of me.

I threw it in the fire.

The Regina Maris came on time, and left again. Captain Marley gave Sister Agnes news from the wicked world. I didn't see him at all.

He snuck in and out, like a thief.

Sister Agnes says that we have a new queen. Eleanor has had her coronation.

Oh.

But her half sister, Catherine, has escaped across the Silken Sleeve and fled to the Continent.

Escaped? Was she a prisoner, too?

Yes, in a way. She lived in her own home, but under guard. After King Edmund died, she wrote secret letters to her friends, asking if they would help her to take the throne from Eleanor.

I began to wonder more about why each of the sisters had been sent to the Island. If I could find out what they had done wrong—or thought about doing wrong—

maybe I would have a better idea about why I was sent here.

Sisters

Barbara Chatwyn

I was Lady of the Bedchamber to Queen Joan.

I stole jewels from her cabinet to pay off my family's debts.

Wynefreed More

While he was fighting for the crown, Edmund tried to rest his troops at our manor.

I locked the door against him!

Philippa Cecil

My husband was Master of the Horse. During a hunt, the king was thrown from his mare, and my husband was accused of plotting it.

I was sent here after his execution.

I certainly learned a great deal from this. Some of the sisters had been very wicked, indeed; some seemed guilty of nothing but bad luck.

I wasn't sure, though, that I had learned anything useful.

Sister Wynefreed and Sister Barbara both had children still living, but those children were not imprisoned like their mothers. Instead, they had sworn loyalty to King Edmund and been allowed to join other noble families.

My parents must have done something much more terrible than Wynefreed or Barbara for me to be sent all the way here. And more terrible than what the Cameron clan had done for me to be sent here alone.

Maybe my father had tried to murder the king.

Maybe my mother was a spy from Gallia or Hispania!

A ship.

It wasn't merely passing by on its way around Albion, or out to the sea.

It was coming toward the Island.

And it was not the *Regina Maris*.

120

Could it be pirates?
A foreign warship?
A plague ship?

No strange ships had ever come to the Island before.

Yet somehow everyone knew what to do.

Bring our bedding to the church, in case we need to sleep there.

Lock and secure every entrance.

Hide the convent records.

Prepare our medical supplies.

Take several days' food up from the cellars.

Plan cold meals.

Gather all the animals to be kept safe in the church.

Haul in fresh water from the well.

Wake Father Ambrose.

Pray!

The longboat was lowered into the bay. It moved slowly.

Maybe the ship was bringing William back.

It was a very silly thought.
I knew it wasn't true.

But I had it, anyway.

I am Sir John Worsley, Baron Hapsworth.

It falls to me to tell you that the pretender to the throne, Lady Eleanor, has been captured at sea, and Her Majesty Queen Catherine has begun her rightful reign.

We sail under Her pennant, and I serve at Her Majesty's pleasure.

Old Kate was queen!

Would she be more forgiving than her father, after all the terrible things that had happened to her? She had lost her title and her mother and her freedom. Surely she wouldn't want to cause those same things to happen to anybody else.

Maybe Sir John had come to tell us that everybody on the Island was—

Pardoned and free!

It was not that I didn't love the Island.

But knowing that I had no choice in living there had changed it from a wonderful place— the only place—

to a grim one.

I did not want to go to Albion, where it seemed even an innocent baby could be hated.

I only wanted to be free so that I would have the Island, my Island—

back again.

Our thanks for bearing us this momentous news, Sir John.

But I am sure you have not come just to tell us this.

Indeed, no.

Her Majesty has charged me to convey these women to your ...safekeeping.

No pardon, then. Or freedom. The new queen had thought of us—

and, instead of granting mercy, was sending new prisoners to live among us and be forgotten, too.

I knew that the Cardinal was the most important priest in Albion. Just like Sister Agnes was the head of our little convent, the Cardinal was the head of all the churches, convents, and monasteries of Albion. And he answered to only two other people on earth:

His Holiness the Pope, who is a bit like a king who rules all the world's churches—

and the King...or Queen...of Albion.

Just meeting the Cardinal would be a great honor. Being sent a letter from him was nearly as important.

Sir John's men went up ahead with Sister Agnes to the Stairway. The girl and I went after them, and the nun walked behind us. The sailors stayed behind.

It gets narrow here. I can go in front of you, if you let go.

No. Next to me.

Or else she will want to walk beside me.

I felt a little bad for her. Mother Mary Clemence certainly didn't seem like a very pleasant travel companion.

So... what should I call you?

You shouldn't.

But then, neither did she.

We all went to the Warming House to dry off—the only room where the hearth is kept lit all day and night in the cold months.

Sir John and his two men went off to look into all the other chambers, with Sister Barbara and Sister Wynefreed following after them. Sister Agnes read the Cardinal's letter.

135

138

I think that was the first moment that I had some idea who the girl was, and how much trouble Mother Mary Clemence was going to be.

But I didn't know for certain until Sister Agnes came to my chamber in the Guest House that night.

Knock Knock

Margaret... may I come in?

Isn't the bell for Vespers about to ring?

I wanted to speak with you before you went to bed.

To thank you for your help today.

140

Normal men, living here? That's not allowed! Where will they sleep? What will they do?

The Cardinal has given his special permission for it, as has the head of our order.

They will share the last chamber in this hall. Her Reverence will supervise them at all times.

So if Mother Mary Clemence tells you to do something, you have to do it.

Often that will be true, yes.

But you're the Prioress! Can't you do anything?

Our guest's well-being is very important.

More important than everyone else's?

Time works differently inside a convent than it does on regular land, or even the way it works at sea.

It's not that it goes faster or slower (although it might seem slower to some people). We just have our very own set of hours. They're religious hours.

Captain Marley had a wonderful thing called a watch. It's a clock small enough to fit in his hand, not like the big hourglass in Sister Agnes's study, or the notched candles that Sister Barbara makes, and certainly smaller than the stone circle.

Has a spring inside.

Tip it over and it takes the sand half an hour to flow through.

Burns through one notch every hour the candle is lit.

I had never known that hours could be reduced to simple **numbers**—

as if they were the hens we counted each night before closing the coop!

Not only that, but they had to **share** a number with another hour on the opposite side of the day. The first eleven o'clock was very different from the later eleven o'clock!

In the convent, we have only eight hours that matter. Each hour is holy, and each hour has its very own name.

At the beginning of every holy hour, we stop working and say a set of prayers, or sing psalms, which are holy songs.

A sister rings the bell before the new hour starts, so you have time to finish whatever you're doing and get ready.

NOCTURNS happens at midnight. This hour makes you ready for the end of the world coming someday, which is supposed to be like being woken up in the middle of the night. I'm asleep for it, or I should be.

COMPLINE is when I go to bed. Some of the saints thought that going to sleep is a little like dying (!), so this is the time to think about people who have died and to pray for their souls.

VESPERS is at sunset. It's a Major Hour, which means that everybody, not just the sisters and Father Ambrose, goes into the church to pray and sing.

This is the time to be thankful for the Glory of All Creation, which luckily includes supper!

NONE is late afternoon. This is the hour of day that the Sorrowful Son died. It wouldn't be very kind to keep working after that happened, so instead it's time to rest or bathe.

LAUDS is a Major Hour. Most times it's right before dawn, and we all wake up and go straight into the church. LAUDS is when you give thanks for light, not just from the sun, but also the light from God. Maud gets up even before Lauds to bake bread. I like to call that time MAUDS.

PRIME is the time before we eat breakfast. I spend it doing chores in the kitchen with Tess if it's a cold month, or at the farm with Sister Philippa if it's warm.

ETIAM

oui

ja

Nai

TERCE is mid-morning. This is the hour that the Sorrowful Son's followers discovered a miracle. Tongues of flame floated over their heads that allowed them to speak and understand any language!

Unfortunately it hasn't happened to me, so I spend this time learning languages from Sister Sybil.

SEXT is in the exact middle of the day. I work on my embroidery with the sisters.

Whenever anybody came to visit the convent, they were supposed to come pray in the church at Lauds and Vespers. Even Sir John's awful guards came. (Their names were Harold Carpenter and Peter Yarrow.)

But Eleanor—Queen Eleanor or Lady Eleanor or whatever she was—did not. Neither did Mother Mary Clemence.

Instead, Father Ambrose was sent up to the Guest House (wheezing all the way) to give them a private service.

And while Mother Mary Clemence came to breakfast and supper with us—and stuck her nose in every other part of the convent—

I must taste the food first, to be certain it is not poisoned.

Or oversalted.

The foul odors of the farm are a disturbance to us as we rest in our chamber. The animals will be moved.

I correspond with many important members of the church in Albion, and my reports must remain secret. You will give up your study to me.

Eleanor did not leave the chamber at all. It was the chamber I had shared with William and Lady Cameron, and where Lady Cameron had died. I wondered if anybody had told Mother Mary Clemence that or if she had simply picked out the biggest room.

Mother Mary Clemence slept there as well, instead of in the dorter with the other sisters.

At Lauds, Tess would take away their chamber pot and last night's supper dishes.
At Prime, Father Ambrose came to say a private Mass for them.
At Terce, Bess would bring up their breakfasts.
At Sext, I would bring up a washbasin of rosewater and take the breakfast dishes.
At None, Father Ambrose returned to lead them in evening prayers,
And at Vespers, Bess brought their supper and took away the wash water.

Either Mother Mary Clemence would open the door, or, if she was out (pestering the sisters, or writing letters to Very Important People who would not receive them for months and months), we would leave anything we brought on a little stool by the door.

One of the guards was always standing by the door. The other would go around with **Her Reverence**—except during Lauds and Vespers, when both men went to join prayers in the church.

Have you seen Eleanor at all?

No! I fear Her Reverence has murdered her!

Don't be silly.

Father Ambrose sees them both twice a day.

I decided to investigate.

Father Ambrose? Have you spoken with... Lady Eleanor?

Who?

The girl. The red-haired girl who came recently.

Ah, you mean Margaret? Where's she gone off to now?

149

I couldn't think of a way to convince Mother Mary Clemence to let Eleanor out of her chamber, or to let me in. And of course Sister Agnes couldn't (or wouldn't) do anything. I shouldn't have worried, though. Eleanor had her own idea almost right away.

Although now I know that that should have worried me even more.

The next evening, Tess brought back the breakfast dishes that had been taken up to Eleanor's chamber.

She didn't eat a bite!

Not fancy enough for her, I suppose.

And the next morning, Tess brought in the previous night's supper dishes.

Still not a bite.

What did Mother Mary Clemence say?

I didn't dare tell her! I just took the dishes and smiled at the guard. Peter.

And the next evening.

We must tell Sister Agnes.

Her Reverence has made it quite clear that the Lady Eleanor is her charge.

Suggesting that anything like this might have escaped Her Reverence's notice would be ill-advised.

I didn't understand at all. Was Eleanor sick? Was Mother Mary Clemence starving her? It was two days before I had another chance to talk to Eleanor. This time I went with Jess.

Gruel is a kind of porridge, but not the good kind.

A Terrible Recipe for Terrible Gruel
(it's terrible!)

- 1 part OATS (normally for the horse)
- 1 part DRIED PEAS (normally for the chickens)
- 1 part WARM WATER or SKIMMED MILK

Directions: Soak everything until soft.
Then mash with a spoon until
disgusting. Do not sweeten
or season. Eat with caution.

158

Mother Mary Clemence made us watch as Lady Eleanor ate the rest of the gruel, then sent us away.

That night Eleanor's supper dishes came back without a scrap left on them.

Over the next two days, Eleanor stayed in the chamber and continued to eat her food. But nobody sent for me. I knocked on the door, once, but nobody answered.

Maybe Eleanor had changed her mind about needing company.

Or about needing my company, anyway.

Maaaaah!

On the third morning, I woke up at sunrise for Lauds, as always.

I dressed and went to church and then helped Sister Philippa milk the goats.

I had breakfast in the kitchen and did some chores there, then went to change my clothes for lessons—

You, girl. Come in right away.

What? Let go!

She's been waiting for you.

Now I know that she was lonely, and afraid I wouldn't come back if she didn't have an important secret to tempt me with.

But right then I only thought that she was very strange and a little cruel and I almost regretted agreeing to visit her.

When I was brought to the chamber the next day, Mother Mary Clemence was there.

Tomorrow you will dine in the Refectory. There will be no more privacy or special treatment at your meals.

The Prioress will report to me on every bite you take.

I am the daughter of a king. I do not share a butter dish with my enemies!

Eleanor didn't say much more than that, and soon Her Reverence left us, looking very satisfied. Had Mother Mary Clemence truly broken Eleanor's spirit? Or was Eleanor secretly pleased that, in the end, she was being allowed out of the chamber?

Maybe that had been her plan all along. I wasn't foolish enough to ask her.

She was the one with questions.

Is supper in the Refectory any better than dining with Her Reverence?

Well...it's a little boring, really. I like it better when I eat in the kitchen.

If you eat in the Refectory, you have to be silent for the whole meal.

Then how do you ask somebody to pass the salt if the fish is bland?

And the fish will be bland.

Table

You use...

These are silent hand gestures that every Elysian sister learns! Sister Sybil says some of them may even be hundreds of years old.

For **honey**, pretend you have some stuck on your thumb, and then lick it away. (Mmm.)

Our **bread** loaves are round, so make a circle with your thumb and forefinger.

If you want **vinegar**, make a sour face—just as sour as vinegar tastes!

This one can be easy to mix up with the sign for honey, so look out.

Signs!

Does the food need any salt?
Just pretend to sprinkle some.

If you'd like some fish,
all you have to do is hold
your breath and swim for it!

Who loves cheese
more than a mouse?

We have to milk the goats
every morning, so it isn't hard
to do it again at the table.

Those are the important ones.

There are plenty of others, though, depending on what's for supper.

I may starve to death after all.

We practiced the table signs for the whole afternoon.

Before I had the chance to ask her about William, it was suppertime.

I w—

!!!

168

The rest of the meal went well enough. Eleanor remembered almost all her signs. (She only poured a little honey on her fish.) Sister Agnes read a long passage of scripture out loud for us, which is the only kind of talking that's allowed, but even though we were all perfectly silent, nobody heard a word.

Supper seemed as though it lasted for hours. Finally the dishes were cleared away, and the sisters went off to say their Compline prayers. Peter Yarrow took us back upstairs.

Do you know how to play chess, Margaret?

I've read about it, but the sisters aren't allowed to play.

Games are a distraction from work and prayer.

But you're not a sister.

Someday I will be.

But you still have time to learn chess and play it with me.

I'm too tired from that meal now, but come by tomorrow and I'll teach you.

And you'll tell me about William?

After that, the hours of my day were never the same.

Some days I wasn't sent for at all, and I only saw Eleanor in the Refectory. Other days, Harold Carpenter or Peter Yarrow would fetch me from the kitchen before Terce, and instead of going to study with Sister Sybil, I would stay in Eleanor's chamber all day.

The next several times I was brought to the chamber, Mother Mary Clemence was there—and she did not leave us alone at all except to use the necessarium. She read us very boring things she had written, mostly about—

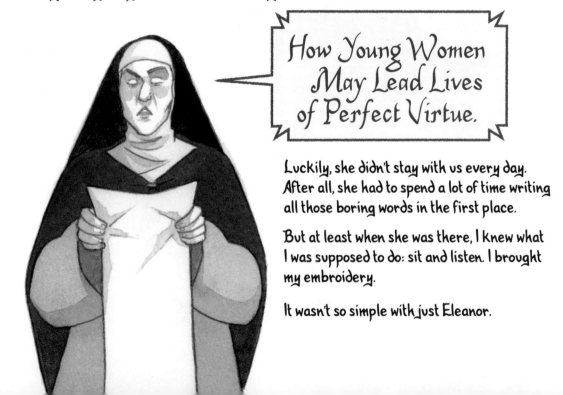

How Young Women May Lead Lives of Perfect Virtue.

Luckily, she didn't stay with us every day. After all, she had to spend a lot of time writing all those boring words in the first place.

But at least when she was there, I knew what I was supposed to do: sit and listen. I brought my embroidery.

It wasn't so simple with just Eleanor.

The first day that we had to ourselves, Eleanor played the lute and told me funny stories about a duchess's pet monkey at the royal court in Albion.

It would hop on ladies' shoulders and steal their earrings, and then hide them inside an old boot.

When a servant found his little treasure trove, all the noble children at court held a trial for the monkey. They found him guilty and sentenced him to death.

172

the Pawn

A foot soldier who has left his farm and family to fight for his kingdom. At the start of the battle, he will charge two spaces, but then he becomes more cautious and only moves **one**.

His pike is long but his arms are short, so he can only defeat a piece in the space across from him.

Each side has eight.

the Rook

Not a single soldier—but a **siege tower**, made of wood and set on iron wheels.

Archers at the top fire arrows over the enemy's walls

or throw down a plank and climb across them.

Because of its wheels, a rook can only move in straight lines.

Each side has two.

the Bishop

Each kingdom has one bishop who only sets foot on white spaces...

and one who only travels across red.

Perhaps they've quarreled over a church matter.

the Knight

He gallops around the field on his mighty warhorse, but he often yanks at the reins. He can only charge two spaces ahead before his steed bucks to the side!

Each side has two.

the King

The last piece is... the **Queen,** whom you've already met.

There is only one queen for each king, of course, and she does not even have a lady-in-waiting to keep her company.

But even alone, she is the kingdom's greatest defender, the cleverest and most powerful of the pieces that move across the board.

And how does she move?

Red squares? White squares?

Straight lines? Diagonals?

A queen...

can go anywhere.

So we played chess, every day.

I tried to keep my pieces out of danger. Eleanor said that whenever one piece defeated another, the losing piece was taken prisoner and executed. I decided that my pieces were more merciful than that. They simply convinced them that it was wrong to fight.

I lost the first few games, but that wasn't unexpected, since I was still only learning. But after a week, I still lost every game. And Eleanor still told me nothing about William. It was the same the week after that.

Eleanor and her Red Queen were very good at setting traps. I thought about all the pawns and knights and bishops and queens and kings she had taken. They had all died because I couldn't play well enough.

But Eleanor refused to do anything else with me until I won a game.

As I lay in bed that night, I realized that the highest cost of winning the game and saving my little kingdom wasn't the death of my pawn—

it was that

I had forgotten

to ask about

William.

I decided I would ask Eleanor about him the next morning.

But the next day, Mother Mary Clemence was in the chamber. She had an illness called gout, which makes your foot hurt and, in her case, makes you even more awful than usual.

Oh! Quiet your voice, child. I feel it down to my toes when you speak.

But I didn't say anything yet.

Perhaps Her Reverence will be more comfortable if we leave her and take a walk around the convent.

183

You said that if I won, you'd tell me about William at Highwall Keep—

We can't speak of it with the guard here. He might report it to Her Reverence, and she would write to Highwall and have your friend punished.

Harold Carpenter certainly was the sort to tell Mother Mary Clemence everything.

I wished Peter Yarrow had been our guard that day, instead. Peter Yarrow ate his meals in the kitchen and listened to Jess tell fairy tales while he peeled turnips for Maud.

Harold Carpenter always took his trencher and ate alone, and he never did anything except what Mother Mary Clemence told him to.

It's difficult to describe somebody you love.
You know how seeing their face makes you feel.

But as for the length of their nose,
or the exact color of their eyes,
you have to think very hard—

because you have to forget who they are
and think only of what a stranger would see.

The more I tried to think of what
William's face looked like,
the harder it became.

186

Oh! There was a painting of you and King Edmund in the church.

I don't know where it is now, though.

Mother Mary Clemence had Sister Barbara take it down.

I can guess which painting it must be a copy of.

Sitting for it was one of the longest times I ever spent with him.

He was disappointed I wasn't a boy, of course.

But you couldn't help that!

He didn't blame me. But it would have made his reign easier to have a male heir.

And, if I had been a boy, he might have taught me to joust and wrestle.

But he was the greatest king in the world;

he had no time to play with dolls.

But the next day, Eleanor invited Sister Sybil to visit us in the chamber; the day after that, Sister Edith; and eventually all the other sisters, too.

Eleanor told Mother Mary Clemence that these were prayer lessons. We would all say a prayer together, so it wasn't really a lie.

And then Eleanor would ask each sister,

Tell me about your crimes against the crown.

They told her the same stories they had told me. The difference was that they told her about King Edmund, too.

194

Eleanor didn't ask to see me for a while after that.
I caught up on my lessons with Sister Sybil, and I worked on my portrait of William.
The sisters and the servants did their best to help.

Before it was finished, Eleanor sent for me again, and we started to walk outside every day. If her feelings had been hurt by everything the sisters had said, it didn't show— or maybe she was just tired of sitting with Mother Mary Clemence.

Walking was a very good idea because Mother Mary Clemence, even when she had set aside her writing and her foot wasn't hurting her, never followed us for long.

Did you think it was a ship coming to take you back to Albion?

I was brought here secretly.

Nobody I care to see even knows I'm here.

If a ship came, it would be to take me to a different prison.

Do you think you'd ever be taken back to Highwall Keep?

Perhaps.

Guard! I'll return to the chamber now.

Mlehhhh!

I felt bad for reminding Eleanor of Highwall Keep. But if she went back and knew for certain what William looked like, she could at least bring him a message from me.

The message would say,

I have not forgotten you.

Margaret! You aren't paying attention.

I'm sorry, Sister.

You are here to learn Latin. Not to draw pictures of William.

I looked down at what I had drawn. It was, for the first time, certainly and absolutely—

...William.

198

The next day I ran to Eleanor's chamber, but she had already gone.

There was no sign of her at the top of the Stairway.

So I climbed down it.

You're to meet her by the cliff steps. It's Yarrow's day to chase her about.

Eleanor hadn't visited the beach since she'd arrived. I thought that Mother Mary Clemence might have forbidden it.

I wondered what she was doing there now.

Look how many seals are on the rock!

I thought I saw a white one. The rest are all black and brown. Is it rare?

I realized then that if Eleanor was going to answer my questions about William, there was nowhere more private than the coracle. If it were just the two of us, nobody could possibly overhear us but the seals and the gulls. It was very clever of her.

202

203

Ah!!

I never saw your little friend, Margaret! I don't need his portrait to know that.

Do you know why?

Because I saw **nobody** at Highwall Keep. I was kept in the same cell, every day and every night, and the **only** face I saw was Mother Mary Clemence's, laughing at my **misery!**

After the ship I had escaped on was captured and boarded by Catherine's privateers, I wrote letters to every friend I had, or thought I had— I even wrote a letter to Catherine, begging her to visit me!

But in all my months at Highwall, not a **single** person wrote a reply, not by letter or by secret message.

Is that what you wanted to hear? That I'm well and truly friendless?

So that you could report it back to Mary Clemence in exchange for some favor?

What? No! I—

Who are you? Who are your parents? Why do you live here?

Don't pretend it's an accident we've been thrown together!

Don't pretend you haven't been worming your way into my confidence since the day I arrived!

I don't know who my parents are. Sister Agnes won't tell me! She took an oath—

You can tell me the truth now, Margaret.

Nobody will overhear us out here on the water.

We're the only two pieces left on the board.

I've always known how to swim. Everybody on the Island does.

It's harder when you're wearing heavy clothes, like Eleanor was, but it's certainly not impossible.

But Eleanor sank— just like Saint Elysia.

Eleanor wasn't exactly a saint, though, so the fish probably weren't going to rescue her.

I would have to do it.

I went to dry off in front of the kitchen fire—if I went to the Guest House I might run into Eleanor again or, worse, Mother Mary Clemence.

Tess was worried that Peter Yarrow would be blamed for letting Eleanor go out in the coracle, and Mother Mary Clemence would—

—send him to prison!

It'd serve him right for not watching the girl, seeing as that's his only duty here.

SOB!

Be gentle, Bess. It's rare that your sister fancies something that the human eye can actually see.

Whatever it was that happened, Maggie, you'd better go to Sister Agnes and tell your side of it.

Right away I started to dread telling Sister Agnes what had happened. Even if I tried to lie to her, it wouldn't work. Nobody would believe that Eleanor went diving in all her clothing on purpose. It would be terrible if Peter Yarrow or Tess were blamed for putting her in danger. Or, worse, what if Eleanor said that I had tried to drown her? What if Mother Mary Clemence was speaking with Sister Agnes this very moment? What if it was already too late? I felt sick.

Her Reverence had taken Sister Agnes's chamber for writing her dreadful letters and books about virtue, but Sister Agnes was still allowed use of it for an hour or two before Vespers.

—absolutely must be sent away from here.

Eleanor!

I wondered why had she come to Sister Agnes herself, instead of sending Mary Clemence to do it?

It might have been a sin to eavesdrop, but if she was telling lies to Sister Agnes about Peter or Tess, it was a good deed to find out and warn them—

Margaret does not remain on the Island simply because I wish her to, milady.

The reason she is here is one that not even Her Reverence could influence.

Then tell me who she is,

or I will tell Her Reverence that Margaret tried to assassinate me today,

and she will have the girl locked up in her chamber for the next five years.

Very
well.

It said that His Majesty had married a woman in secret.

His last wife was not a foreign princess, or even a high-ranking noblewoman of Albion.

She was the widow of a merchant, hardly what the kingdom expected of a queen.

Margaret, the child I now held in my arms, was their daughter—an unexpected child, since her mother had had no children with her past husband.

The kingdom nearly tore itself in half when His Majesty sent away Catherine's mother and married yours, milady.

He had reason to fear that this newest wife and child would be in danger from both his enemies and his friends.

So the marriage was kept secret, and Margaret was sent away, to be kept secret and safe—

and there was no place in Albion more secret or safe than here, especially if her identity was hidden from the inhabitants.

Her existence would only be made known to the world if you were to die and make her heir to the throne.

Otherwise she would live here, quietly, as if she were a sailor's orphan, and remain untroubled by the matters of the world.

It can't be true. My father could not have married without anybody finding out.

Some adviser of his would have known. The priest who married them would have known.

Some did, I'm certain. But there would have been no reason to reveal it. And now most of those who knew have probably fled to the continent, or died of the sweating sickness, or been executed by Catherine.

Or are keeping their silence as members of Catherine's court.

And have you seen these marriage papers? Can it be proved at all? Who was this woman?

I have only the letter as proof, and that I have hidden safely.

The marriage could be false, but I see no reason why it should not be true.

The woman is not named.

Since His Majesty's death, Margaret's mother has either died herself, or wisely kept the marriage secret.

Why didn't you tell me this on the very day I arrived?

219

It is well that you think Margaret harmless, outside of a coracle. But your father was hardly more than a child when he first fought to become king.

Catherine was only a child when you were born, and she learned to hate you.

If Catherine keeps the throne... if she learns of Margaret's existence...

...could you guarantee Margaret's safety?

If I had told you when you arrived, you might have informed Mother Mary Clemence, to gain some favor from her.

Snort!

I thought not.

I did not know you well then, but I had guessed enough about Her Reverence to know that she would love to deliver Margaret to her queen, as a prize.

But now you have been friends with Margaret, at least until today.

From William's case, you know how loyal she can be to anybody she calls her friend.

I hope that is enough to convince you not to betray her.

Eleanor didn't call for me to visit her after that. She even took her meals in her chamber. She must have told Mother Mary Clemence that she was unwell. Maybe she really was. I was not certain I would have gone to visit her even if she had asked.

Perhaps she would change her mind about my being a threat to her crown, and push me down the stairs!

Her own sister!

The only thing I knew for certain was that she hadn't told Mother Mary Clemence who I was yet.

Her Reverence ignored me or scolded me just as she had before.

SPLISH!

Sister Agnes also behaved as if nothing had happened, even though she knew that I had heard the entire conversation. I had so many questions I wanted to ask her:

Where was the letter hidden? Had she really told Eleanor everything that was in it, or did it say who my mother was? Did it say why my mother didn't come to the Island with me? Why did Sister Agnes let me listen at all? Was it so I would know to be wary of Eleanor? Would Sister Agnes have ever told me any of those secrets if Eleanor hadn't made threats?

It had been so long since the two of us had truly spoken.

Margaret. Margaret?

Hm?

You've sewn your needlework to your skirt again.

I thought that learning why I was on the Island would answer all my questions. Not make more of them.
The first winter storm rolled toward us over the Silver Sea, but it was nothing compared to the storm in my head.

227

The sisters all went to the church to pray,
leaving me behind to watch.
After nearly an hour of fighting
the waves, the ship tilted, and its
masts plunged down into the waves.

Were the sisters not praying
hard enough? Was Saint Elysia
busy somewhere else?

A longboat!
They put out their
longboat before
they sank!

Sometimes a small boat fares
better than a large one.

If they could only make it
farther into the bay—

It's raising
a flag—

It's mine!

229

After that, there was nothing left to see.

You'll do them no good worrying, Maggie.

Some of them may yet make it through, and they'll appreciate that broth if they do.

But I saw the big ship and the longboat sink! How could anybody survive?

Have I not told you of my own husband's rescue?

231

The Elysian order's duty, once a storm at sea has passed, is to search the shores and the harbor for any survivors in need of hospital care, to find, **bury**, and **pray** for the drowned, and to **provide charity and shelter** to any widows or orphans who remain.

We can't quite do that last part—instead, the sisters send their embroideries back to the order, which sells them and then gives the money to the grieving families.

Sometimes storms will rake across the Silver Sea and bring more to the beach than just weathered logs and seaweed.

I had seen all sorts of things wash up that sailors may have lost overboard, or parts of ships knocked off in a storm.

A wooden recorder.

A drinking cup made of horn.

Three leather shoes, the kind sailors wear.

A glass flask, empty except for a little seawater.

A funny necklace, strung with abalones.

The huge wooden hand of a ship's figurehead.

A cherrywood jewelry box, with no jewels left inside.

But this was very different.

Sister Agnes and Sister Philippa
rowed the coracle out in the bay to make
sure there were no men in the water there.

The rest of us combed the wreckage for
survivors, or for something to tell us what
the ship was, so the families of the dead men
could be told that they were lost.

Why had Eleanor volunteered to help?
It was a good thing to do, of course,
but she had ignored many chances
to do good things.

Maybe she was only curious,
but she wandered around the shore
as if she were looking for something.

Oh.
Sister.

Sister
Edith.

Eleanor had seen the longboat.

She had seen the flag as well, then.
That was why she had come down to the beach.

But she hadn't mentioned the flag at all.
She didn't want the sisters to know.

What would happen
if the guards or the
sisters found out that
the ship was actually
loyal to Eleanor?

She had been brought
here secretly. Not even
Captain Marley knew
that his passenger used
to be a queen.

Eleanor knew who I was,
and I couldn't trust her not
to use that knowledge to
hurt me.

Now I knew something
that could hurt her.

Eleanor may have lied to me and then tried to have me
sent away, but I didn't think she deserved to be punished.
At least not in the ways Her Reverence or Her Majesty
would think up.

What if I told Eleanor about the flag but hid it? I could just threaten to expose
the rescue attempt to Her Reverence unless she kept our sisterhood secret.

That would mean telling Eleanor that I knew
we were sisters, though, and that might put
me in even more danger from her.

It had been less than a week since I'd learned that I had any sisters at all,
and there were already so many ways we could hurt each other.

What I did in the next quarter hour—whose side I chose—could change the future of the whole kingdom. But which choice would end with William being freed from Highwall?

Which queen would pardon the sisters at the convent for their crimes? What would make the Island into the place I thought it was, before I learned the truth?

I felt like I was staring at Eleanor's chessboard again.

Here...

He was still alive.
Only asleep.
But very hot.

I prayed to Saint Elysia to keep him
alive and asleep until I could return.

I prayed to the Merciful Mother to
keep him out of pain and lower his fever.

I prayed to the Sorrowful Son to
keep him from calling out again.

And I prayed to God to help
me decide what to do next.

I pulled the flag back into the sea cave, where it couldn't be seen, and tied it around a rock so the tide couldn't wash it out again.

If the man stumbled toward the outside, maybe he'd see it and guess that I had been real, and not some strange dream, and he would remember to stay in the cave.

I pushed as much of the wrecked longboat as I could down toward the waves, so the tide would take it away sooner.

Did you find anything?

Just some broken timber from the longboat.

I won't tell anyone.

Why not?

There was only one kind of sister I knew how to be, and it wasn't the sort of sister that Eleanor and Catherine were to each other.

It is my duty as a future sister of the Elysian order to help and protect the shipwrecked and the stranded, *always*.

He is shipwrecked. *You* are stranded. So I'll help you. And so will Saint Elysia.

I will be grateful to have Saint Elysia's help in the bargain.

This man. Did he say his name?

Francis.

What were his looks?

Dark hair and a small beard. He didn't sound like a sailor.

The next few days were very strange.

The young man—*Francis Paget, the Earl of Kense*—would have to stay hidden in the cave until he was no longer so feverish that he might give himself away.

Eleanor could not get away from Mother Mary Clemence or the guards. After the coracle, even Peter Yarrow would not let her out of his sight.

So I was the only one who could go to the cave.

I could bring him fresh water without much trouble, but I couldn't get caught taking food from the kitchen, or sneaking bandages from the infirmary, or missing my lessons.

We tore up one of Eleanor's fine linen shifts into strips for bandages. She had the kitchen send food with me when I visited her chamber, and then I would hide it in my apron to take to the cave.

So Eleanor asked for me to keep her company every day, then would send me out on "errands" at low tide, when the mouth of the cave was open.

If Sister Agnes was concerned or surprised by my return to Eleanor's company, she didn't say anything.

253

Eleanor was *almost* sweet to me.

Whether she was trying to show her gratitude for my help, or fear that I might betray her and Francis to Mother Mary Clemence, I couldn't tell.

I kept the scrap of flag in my pocket, just in case.

It turned my fingers red.

There was just one thing that I didn't understand at all.

You said that he betrayed you by coming here.

How?

He's put all three of us in danger, hasn't he?

Now, hurry out, before you miss the tide or **Her Reverence** returns.

Caring for him in secret was dangerous, but the storm was hardly his fault. The ship had come here under her flag, so surely he had come to rescue her.

How could that be a betrayal?

Francis gradually grew better. Once he was dried off, and his cuts and scrapes healed up, he was able to eat and drink a little more. His fever went down, though he was still very pale. He finally realized that I wasn't Eleanor.

I didn't get to visit Francis the next day.

It was Sunday, and Sundays are the quietest day at the convent, when even most chores are set aside in favor of prayer.

The tide was too high the only time I could get away. When I saw him on Monday, something had changed.

I dunked some of the bandages in the cold seawater and laid them on his face and neck to keep him cool.

That was all I knew how to do.

Fever!

Please don't die.

I had a terrible feeling that he *would*, very soon, unless he had better help than me. The tide was coming in, and so was another storm. The water was already rushing up to my ankles at the mouth of the cave. Soon it would be up to my knees, and at the rock wall it would be up to my waist—too strong and cold and dangerous to wade through.

There wasn't time to run and get Eleanor, even if she were free to help me.

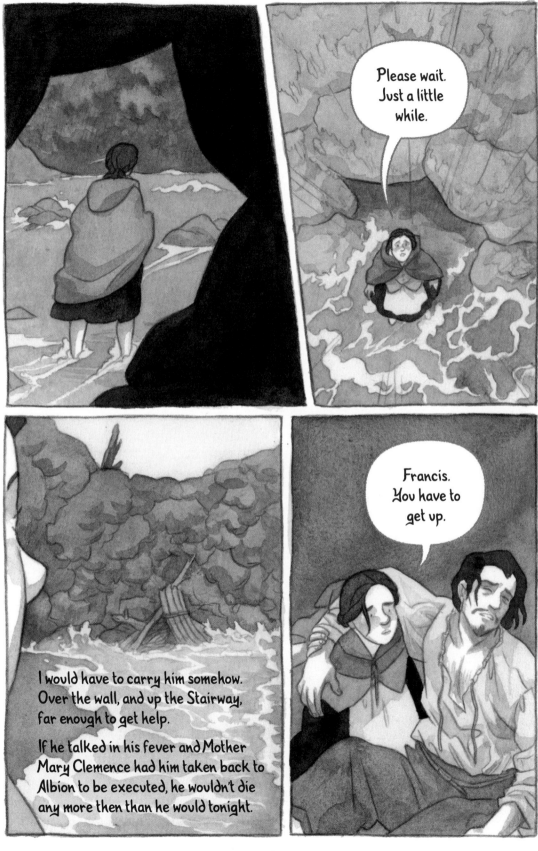

Please wait.
Just a little
while.

Francis.
You have to
get up.

I would have to carry him somehow.
Over the wall, and up the Stairway,
far enough to get help.

If he talked in his fever and Mother
Mary Clemence had him taken back to
Albion to be executed, he wouldn't die
any more then than he would tonight.

Tess had a different explanation, which I liked much better,

although I also found it far more frightening.

Sometimes,

the Queen of the Sea

takes a fancy to a person
she sees on the shore.

Maybe it's a child she recognizes as one of her own,
left behind when last she took to the sea. Maybe it's
a handsome lad whose heart is already spoken for!

But when she does see a person her heart longs for,
and sees them distracted or daydreaming, instead of
coming ashore herself, she may send a great wave
to snatch them up!

You may swim as fast as you like, but even then you
may be swept out to sea, to join her kingdom—
though you may be drowned by the journey.

Those who survive such a wave and are washed
back up to shore are said to have received a
warning that someday the queen will claim
them for her own...

one way or another!

I had never been caught by such a wave myself, though I always looked out at the surf to be sure the Queen of the Sea knew that I was paying attention.

So imagine my surprise when I met one at last.

265

Climbing the Stairway was one of the most horrible things I've ever done in my life.

Cold rain started to pour down on us. At first I was glad, because Francis was so hot with fever and it cooled him a little, and even with our wet clothes I knew that getting us both to the top would eventually turn into sweaty work.

Soon, though, the rain washed away all the warmth we had between us.

Francis started to shake.

If I could get him to the top, I could hide him in the barn with the animals, in the warm, dry hay, and then find Eleanor, and she would decide what to do.

So we climbed.

And we climbed.

There are five hundred

and eighty-seven steps

in the Stairway.

William and I counted them once.

Sometimes I dream that I'm still climbing them.

Come in.

I will say that I found him while walking.

You'll lie to Mother Mary Clemence?

No. I am walking, and I shall find him.

He has a fever. The sweating sickness is still a concern on Albion— we will keep him in quarantine for the time being.

That should do away with any interest Her Reverence might have in visiting him.

When he regains his senses, he may give his own report of how he came to our shores.

Sister Agnes went to quietly fetch Sister Edith and the litter
to bring Francis in with. I sat on the Stairway with him and held
his hand, though I don't know if he could even feel it any longer.

The rain stopped, but it grew darker, and the wind made strange
noises howling up the Stairway.

It took a little doing, but he was in the infirmary before dark,
and nobody had breathed a word about our new patient to
Mother Mary Clemence.

Or to Eleanor.

Sister Edith and Sister Agnes were both in the infirmary as part of Francis's "quarantine," so I heard no news from them. Eleanor didn't come to visit me.

Finally I was well enough again to leave my chamber and have breakfast in the kitchen. Tess told me over breakfast that Sister Edith had lifted the quarantine on the infirmary. I asked if I could bring them the fresh linens.

Good morrow, Margaret.

I'm glad to see you well again.

Sir *Thomas* here was giving us his account of the latest events in Albion before he left on the sad adventure that brought him to us.

Why had Eleanor passed him by so coldly? She didn't call for me, so I had no chance to ask her. I tried to visit Francis on my own, but every time I had a moment to spare, somebody else was already sitting by his side.

Most of the convent found excuses to come and examine the new patient.

277

How did you find out she was here? I thought it was a secret.

There were a great many rumors about where she was taken after Highwall Keep. Some even thought she had died.

I pretended to be loyal to Catherine long enough to find out which of the rumors were more likely to be true.

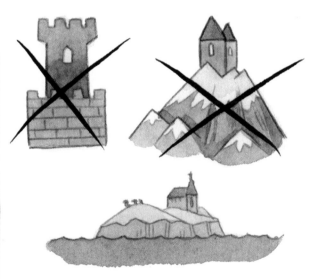

Of the three that seemed possible, this was the only one I had any hope of rescuing her from.

And I could not even do that.

That didn't sound like somebody who had betrayed Eleanor.

It could be worse. You could've died in the shipwreck. At least this way you still get to see her.

Yes, but never alone. And if Her Reverence knew who I really was, she'd have me thrown back into the sea.

I could bring Eleanor a message for you.

No, Mistress Margaret.

That would be dangerous,

and you've risked enough for me already.

281

I wasn't so sure that was true.

Francis was kind and quiet and brave, and he had risked his life to help Eleanor— despite how awful and strange she could be sometimes. If he still wanted her to be queen, surely other people in Albion felt the same way.

Mother Mary Clemence was the opposite of Francis in every way. She had been happy to hear that Catherine had executed or imprisoned so many of her own subjects, as if it were something to be proud of.

What if I had never met Eleanor at all and simply had to pick between a queen chosen by Francis, or a queen chosen by Mother Mary Clemence?

That was an easy question to answer.

But if Eleanor refused to talk to Francis—the one person who might be able to convince her that there was still hope—then there would be no choosing at all. Not for any of us, and not for Albion.

That moment is when Saint Elysia came to the rescue again.

Have you seen Saint Elysia's relic yet?

It's in her chapel. Maybe it will help. You can ask Saint Elysia if Albion really is better off with Old Kate.

Mother Mary Clemence won't come because you'll just be praying, and the guard will have to wait outside anyway. I'll go with you after Vespers!

What harm can it do?

There are many, many saints, of course. Saint Elysia isn't the only one.

Saints are mostly people who once walked around and ate breakfast and put their shoes on one at a time, just like you or me. They did something amazing enough that instead of just going to heaven after they die, they become messengers to heaven!

Not everybody gets to be a saint through miracles and good deeds, like Saint Elysia. Some saints died while bravely defending their faith.

Those saints are called **martyrs**.

Martyrs have died in all kinds of awful ways. If something terrible happens to you, it's probably not as bad as being eaten by lions, like Saint Leonisius was.

And if you are being eaten by lions, you know that Saint Leonisius understands.

I certainly do!

After someone becomes a saint, she sits in heaven and listens to the prayers of living people, and tries to help them. You can choose to pray to a saint who had a problem like yours when they were alive. Or you can pray to a saint who performed the kinds of miracles you're hoping will happen to you—like curing a sickness or surviving a storm at sea.

Praying to a saint, or doing something else to honor them, is called **venerating**. You can also pray to a saint in a place that was important to them. Some people think that makes it more likely that a saint will hear you.

Something else that can help you get even closer to a saint is a **relic**. Holy relics are things that used to belong to saints, or important objects that they touched—sometimes they're even **parts** of saints!

You wouldn't think that a small place like the Island would have a relic of its own. But you would be wrong. Because we possess...

Saint Elysia's Fish Head!

It's the head of one of the fish that saved Saint Elysia from drowning!

And how does a humble convent come to have such a thing?

Saint Elysia was rescued by a whole **school** of fish.

Other Elysian convents have a whole fish, and some only have a single bone. But they're all holy!

I look forward to seeing it, then—

I went to sit in the choir,

to make sure that the guard
didn't come in and find them.

But I didn't have to worry.
Harold Carpenter was fast asleep outside.

It was hours yet until the sisters would come
in for their next prayers. The church smelled
of beeswax and dust and smoke and old wood.

It seemed as though even the Sorrowful Son
was fast asleep in his mother's arms.

Had I ever slept in my mother's arms?

Consider it your punishment for deceiving us.

So you haven't given up? You'll try to be queen again?

We shall see.

Eleanor's plan for spending time with Francis turned out to be very clever. The next day, she told Her Reverence,

I sorely miss the company of young persons equal to my rank and find I grow fractious under the surveillance of my guards.

(Translation: Eleanor missed talking to other young people who spent most of their time in palaces, unlike me, and the guards were getting on her nerves.)

And then:

Sir Thomas is a man of discretion and valor, and you can have no objection to his loyalties.

He shall inform me of all the changes Her Royal Highness has wrought on Albion, and I cannot but take moral instruction from his accounts.

(Translation: "Sir Thomas" was very proper, and since he was supposed to be loyal to Queen Catherine, he would spend all his time convincing Eleanor that Kate made a better queen after all.)

We shall avail ourselves of the curative sea air, so as to remain robust in our confinement.

(Translation: They'd walk around in the cold and wet for exercise, which Mary Clemence and her sore foot would absolutely hate.)

I shall require a chaperone, of course.

The maid, Margaret, has fulfilled the role of lady's companion sufficient to judge propriety, and her unfailing honesty cannot be questioned.

(Translation: I would walk around with them to make sure they got into no mischief, and I could be trusted to give Mother Mary Clemence a truthful report of what they did.)

293

In other words,

I would have to lie.

The Library on the Island doesn't have very many exciting books.

There are mostly books of prayers, books **about** prayers, and books that teach you languages (so you can pray in them). Only a few of them have good stories. There is exactly one book about love— the kind that you fall into, anyway.

The book is about a knight and a noble maiden.

Even though they're in love, they never ever touch, and they certainly don't **kiss**. They hardly even get to speak to each other, because their families have promised to marry them to other people.

The closest they get is when the maiden drops her kerchief, and he picks it up but doesn't give it back to her. He **knows** that she meant for him to keep it, even though she never said.

(Personally, I would be angry if somebody kept **my** kerchief without asking permission, because the embroidery on it took a very long time.)

The maiden becomes very sick, and is about to die, because she's so sad that she can never marry the knight. The only cure is for her to smell a holy rose that grows on top of a mountain far away.

The knight rides through a winter storm and defeats a **whole army** and walks over a bridge of fire that burns his feet, all to get the rose.

He finally returns and brings the rose to her in time. She breathes the rose and is cured, but then he dies at her feet because of all his wounds!

After that, the maiden becomes a nun. (That's the way a lot of stories about maidens end.)

She spends the rest of her life praying for the knight's soul to go to heaven.

I always thought the story was silly.

If that was love, then I was glad that I lived in a convent, where you didn't have to worry about it.

If the girl had just gone straight to the convent at the very beginning, maybe the knight would have lived a long life.

Sister Sybil told me that the book isn't really about the **marrying** kind of love.

It's about loving God so much that you'd give up everything you have, or do terrible and frightening things, or even die, like the saints, if God told you it was the right thing to do.

But I still think it's a silly book.

I spent a good part of the winter months walking six feet ahead of, or behind, Eleanor and Francis. Sometimes the weather was too bad for walking and Mother Mary Clemence was in bed with her gouty foot up. Then we sat in the Warming Chamber together while Eleanor played songs on her lute for us, or Francis and Eleanor played chess while I embroidered.

When the weather was good, we would go down to the waves and walk. Twice we went skating on the pond. Francis was very good at it. Eleanor wasn't. He didn't say so.

It isn't natural for mortals to walk on water.

It's supposed to be a miracle, not something to do for sport.

Your Majesty is no normal mortal.

If I could perform such a miracle, I would have walked home to Albion long ago.

Born to rule an island nation, yet she can neither skate on ice nor swim through water.

Though perhaps I could learn that, too, when the thaw comes.

But at least twice a week they would have one of their **secret conversations.** That's when I had to stand a ways away and make sure nobody was coming near who might overhear them.

...great danger. She may move against the Cardinal....demand an oath of loyalty from all the abbeys and priories ....destroy the rest...

...nonsense. My father would never have spent the kingdom's money so recklessly.

...treaty with the Hollish king— there's even...that Catherine might marry his son...

Albion would be under Hollish rule within a fortnight!

...easier to surrender. The shame of my defeat... be happy with what is left to me.... ...live the ordinary life of a king's unrecognized child...

I had never seen a man and a woman kiss. In fact, the only kissing I'd seen at all was Father Ambrose kissing us in church as part of the benediction, but that was *holy*.

I thought Francis was loyal to Eleanor as his queen. How could he *kiss* her? And how could she say that she would give up the throne? I thought he had risked his life to give her the chance to be queen again!

Had Francis lied to me? Had he come here like the knight bringing his rose? Had they kissed in Saint Elysia's chapel while I looked out for them?

Kissing was certainly and absolutely not allowed there. Saint Elysia would be furious!

And what would happen if Mother Mary Clemence caught them?

Terrible things, and I would be punished right along with them!

And I could be queen. I could tell Mother Mary Clemence everything they'd done and who Francis really was, and have them both sent away (though I would make sure they weren't executed), and I would be taken back to Albion as a hero. Then I would slip away and find my mother, who would be so happy to see me and would have proof that she and King Edmund had been married, so I was the crown princess!

Then I would reveal my true identity to the whole kingdom, and all the people of Albion would realize how good a queen I would be. They'd get rid of Old Kate right away. I would let William out of prison, and I would pardon all the sisters at the convent for their crimes. Eventually I would pardon Francis and Eleanor, but only after they apologized in front of the whole kingdom. If they didn't, they could live on the Island forever and clean out the barn every day until they forgot all about *kissing*!

All Hail Queen Margaret!

The next day, Eleanor sent word for me to meet her in Saint Elysia's chapel.

Francis was not there. Peter Yarrow was her guard and looked at me very nervously as I went into the church. No doubt he was worried that I might tell Maud about his meeting Jess in the cellar.

At least it meant that he wasn't likely to bother us.

That kind of love is not allowed for royalty.

When we marry, our kingdom is married as well.

We must love for our kingdom and not for ourselves.

I thought about King Edmund and my mother. Eleanor must have been thinking about them, too. At least one king had loved and married for himself.

But their love had been kept a secret, and maybe this was the reason.

So I have not... thought about love any more than a sister at a convent would.

Maybe I have always loved Francis and did not know it until now.

Or maybe I have never loved him at all—

perhaps I'm only grateful that he finds me worth loving.

I don't understand.

Margaret, when you fought with me over the fate of your friend,

I think I was... jealous of your love for him.

I don't want to marry William, though.

I only want him to be safe, and near me again.

But you love him as if he were your brother. A brother worth loving. I would...I would wish for you to love me that way, too.

Just as I wish for Francis to love me, though in a different way.

I have not always behaved well toward you, or to Francis,

because I don't know how to act to make a single person love me, instead of a whole kingdom.

But despite that, you have been as generous as...as a sister should be.

Everything around me suddenly felt very sharp and alive. Eleanor was going to tell me herself that we were sisters—actual sisters—and that she wanted me to come with her when she left the Island, whether through royal pardon or escape.

Before that moment, every time I thought about leaving the Island, it was just a silly fantasy. Before I knew that I was King Edmund's daughter, I hadn't really thought of it at all, even when William talked about showing me Castle Cameron someday. It would have felt the same if he had talked about showing me a castle at the bottom of the sea.

At that moment, though, my heart started to beat faster, and I held my breath, and for some reason I thought,

Take me with you.

So, from now on, regardless of who may love whom, I will do everything I can to protect you.

Especially from Her Reverence, who would hurt my friends whenever she cannot hurt me.

I owe you that much, and more.

Now you should go, before the sisters come in for their prayers.

Eleanor still wanted to keep her secrets.

313

But do you wish to marry her?

If she said she would give up being queen to marry you, would you let her?

...Yes.

I fear that I might.

I wasn't sure why Francis was frightened. The knight wasn't frightened by all the terrible things he faced to bring the rose to his maiden.

Francis had already risked his life to find Eleanor.

What could possibly scare him now?

Francis did know that if Eleanor gave up forever on being queen because she loved him, then Catherine would stay the ruler of Albion.

Everything that happened to the kingdom because of Catherine would really be his fault—for letting Eleanor fall in love with him.

That could be frightening, in a way.

Of course, I knew something that Francis didn't. Eleanor and I were sisters. Eleanor thought she was keeping our sisterhood a secret from me. After all, I might try to steal her kingdom, too—or side with Catherine against her.

Like Sister Agnes said, children can be dangerous. As long as I, and everyone else, thought I was just an ordinary orphan, I could never get in the way of Eleanor's plans.

But what if Eleanor told me who I really was, and trusted that I wouldn't betray her? What if she brought me back to Albion with her? King Edmund had married my mother after both Queen Joan and Queen Isabel had died. As long as Sister Agnes had her letter, nobody could argue that I was born out of wedlock.

That wasn't true of Eleanor—or of Catherine, either. I was the one daughter of Edmund that all of Albion could agree on! Once everyone knew about me, Catherine would have to admit defeat. Eleanor would get to marry Francis. Both would give up their right to the throne. And I would become the true queen of Albion.

Eleanor could teach me everything I needed to know about ruling a kingdom. It would be just like playing chess together—only, we would be on the same side of the board!

But it seemed as though Eleanor didn't just want to save Albion from Catherine. She wanted to save it by being the *queen*.

Eleanor had taught me that a queen is the most valuable piece on the chessboard.

You can sacrifice almost any other piece without feeling too badly—there will always be plenty of pawns, and at least one other knight, rook, or bishop.

Although a queen is very powerful, any piece can capture her if she's careless. And you only have one queen. You can lose very quickly if she is captured too soon in the game.

I lost half a dozen chess games to Eleanor or Francis because I was so worried about keeping my queen safe that I hardly used her at all. The other side won—not by being responsible, but by being reckless!

But there is a special move in chess.

If a pawn can creep safely all the way to the other end of the board without getting caught—

—it becomes
a new queen.

It is much easier to win when you have two queens
and your opponent only has one.

I wished I knew how to convince
Eleanor that we were on the same side.

All I could do was pray for Saint Elysia to send me an idea.

Margaret! Why is your hand bloody?

Oh. Sebastian bit me. The scab fell off.

Here. Stop it before you bleed all over your work.

This is too pretty to use as a bandage.

Don't be foolish.

JE SAIS QUI JE SUIS. JE SAIS

JE SAIS QUI J

"Je Sais Qui Je Suis." That's in Gallish.

I don't know that either, but I could learn it—

Which family rules the kingdom of Lettovia?

How do you prevent a famine in the kingdom after a drought year?

How many lords of *Ecossia* participated in the last rebellion against the crown?

How do you address an ambassador from *Almagribbe* without causing offense?

You can't be queen, Margaret.

You would only put yourself in danger, and the kingdom, too.

The *Regina Maris* was almost six weeks early.

It normally didn't come until after the Paschal Feast.

The forty days leading up to the week of the feast are very quiet and spare.

Nobody, not even the servants, is allowed to eat any rich foods, or play any games, or sing anything but holy songs.

On some days the adults are supposed to fast— that means only eating one small meal for the whole day.

I used to wish I could join in the fasting.

It made me feel like a baby, and William, too, to eat my porridge while everybody else was so grown up and holy.

After that flavorless month, the Paschal Feast arrives, and all the best food appears on the supper table again. Since the *Regina Maris* comes shortly afterward with half a year's worth of fresh supplies, Sister Wynefreed and Maud can empty the cellars without concern.

But the ship coming early meant that there was a lot of work to do, very quickly.

Suddenly the whole Island was busy. Tess and Bess hurried to ready a room in the Guest House for Captain Marley and to start the meal we'd feed to the sailors.

329

330

Soon the *Regina Maris* had reached the bay, and it was time for everybody to go down the Stairway to the dock to meet the longboat. I was sent to fetch Francis, and soon I realized the worst thing of all about the ship's early arrival.

I must leave the Island earlier than I thought.

Couldn't you say that you're still not feeling well enough to sail, and stay here on the Island until the fall?

If I were really Sir Thomas, I would be eager to return to court. Her Reverence would become very suspicious.

You'll be in trouble if you just go back to Albion, won't you? Somebody might recognize you, and you could be sent to Highgate Keep, or...worse!

I will travel as Sir Thomas and then become Francis Paget again only after I safely arrive— I still have a few friends who would help me to flee Albion.

Then I will try to convince the people of a foreign land to send another ship here.

333

The *Regina Maris* had never brought more than two new people at a time.
It's hard enough to feed just one extra person for half a year without any warning.
Six new women and no extra supplies meant that—

Meals might become very skimpy.

You'll have your wish at last to join in the fasting, Margaret.

Sir Thomas is departing—we can feed two women on his rations.

Who were all these new women? Prisoners, of course.

Some were like Lady Cameron and the sisters—noblewomen whose families weren't loyal enough to the crown. Queen Catherine had found all sorts of new enemies, it seemed. But some of them were already nuns.

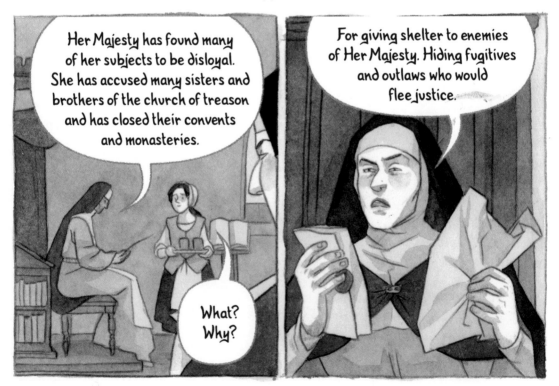

Her Majesty has found many of her subjects to be disloyal. She has accused many sisters and brothers of the church of treason and has closed their convents and monasteries.

What? Why?

For giving shelter to enemies of Her Majesty. Hiding fugitives and outlaws who would flee justice.

But if a person comes to a convent and asks for protection, you're supposed to let them in, no matter who they are.

Treason is a sin. A much greater sin than turning away vagabonds.

They should have locked their doors or turned over these criminals to the Royal Guard.

Many sisters and brothers have been sent to prisons to await trial. The holy sisters who arrived here today are among them.

And the convents and monasteries that were closed have been turned into barracks for Her Majesty's soldiers.

I've already told you about martyrs.

Saints who sacrificed their lives for a holy cause. And I've already told you that Saint Elysia wasn't a martyr. But that's because nobody ever even saw her die!

One misty day she went out in a fishing boat— a coracle, like ours—to visit the fishermen who made their living on the waves.

After she had spoken with the last fisherman, she began to row away. But she didn't row back to shore, as he expected she would. Instead she started to row out to sea. When he asked where she was going, she answered,

> I have visited the fishermen.
> Now it's the fishes' turn.

There are some versions of the story where she turned into a fish and swam away, but even I think that's a little ridiculous.

There's another version where Saint Elysia rowed away into the mist and was never seen again, at least not by anybody who already knew her.

Sometimes people say they've been rescued from drowning, or warned off of sailing onto rocks, or saved from being captured by pirates, by an Elysian sister in a coracle who rowed away before they could thank her.

I like that story better.

Traitor Fujitive

The letter that Mother Mary Clemence had received not only had a picture of Francis drawn on it but also a description of him and a list of all the crimes he had committed—or that Queen Catherine said he had committed. Theft, spying, conspiracy, treason!

Francis had hoped that nobody in Albion would notice he was gone until after he had already found and rescued Eleanor and they had escaped to the Continent. But the shipwreck meant that he'd been trapped here for too long. Everybody in court had had time to realize that he had disappeared for good, and to discover that he'd stolen money from the Royal Treasury—enough to buy a ship and to hire soldiers to help him rescue Eleanor.

The letter said that Francis might be anywhere—in Gallia, or Ecossia, or even just hiding in Albion in disguise. It said that Francis knew enough from his time pretending to be loyal to Queen Catherine that he might have guessed that Eleanor was on the Island. He might try to come here. If he did, Mother Mary Clemence should have her men take him prisoner immediately, so he could be taken back to Albion on the first ship.

Nobody knew that he was already here.
Except for us.

Now we were guilty of treason, too.

Mother Mary Clemence couldn't be quite sure yet who "we" were, though. Eleanor obviously knew that "Sir Thomas" was really Francis. And Francis, of course, knew who he was.

If I had just stood there and pretended to be surprised, Mother Mary Clemence might not have guessed that I knew, too.

She might've kept thinking I was just a silly little girl who played Cherry Pit and daydreamed while Eleanor and Francis whispered plots to each other just a few feet away. At the very least she would've had to go get her awful Liar's Taper.

Instead, I ran.

Catch her, Carpenter!

Stop him!

339

344

We ran up the stairs and into the Guest House. I'm not sure where I thought we'd go after we found Eleanor. I'm not sure Francis knew, either.

The only thing that mattered was reaching Eleanor before Mother Mary Clemence did.

Is Lady Eleanor within?

Yes, milord. Do you come to take her out for your last stroll before they send you home?

Yes. We shall look after her.

You may leave for the kitchens, if you wish.

Yes, milord. No doubt they could use my help there.

345

Mother Mary Clemence locked us all into separate rooms.

Eleanor in her bedchamber.

Francis in the little room where the guards had their beds.

My cell in the dorter and the spare chambers in the Guest House were occupied by the women who had arrived on the *Regina Maris*, so I was taken back to Sister Agnes's cell.

Mother Mary Clemence locked the door behind her without saying a word.

Hours went by.

But the church bells didn't ring, and I didn't hear the sisters singing from the cloister or the dorter on their way into the church, the way they should've.

The glass in the window wasn't clear enough to see anything through. And everything that might have been useful in the room had been taken away. Even the fire had been put out, which meant that the room grew colder and darker by the minute.

Who told you that—Eleanor? The *people* have already half forgotten that she was ever queen, and they will forget about her completely in a few years' time.

After a few years in the dungeon, she may forget *herself*.

As for the sisters, and the servants,

I cannot prove that any of them knew Sir Thomas was the Earl of Kense.

But my man Carpenter reported their actions today in helping you.

The servants will be sent back to Albion and punished in the stockade. The sisters will do all their own work from now on.

The sisters are already prisoners, of course, but they may not be so bold when their yearly rations from Albion are cut in half and no new animals or goods are brought to them ever again. They will slowly starve to death, over the course of years, until this Island is as empty as the day it came out of the sea.

And me?

You?
Why should I even bother to punish *you*, Margaret?

You are as powerless as a flea, and worth just as little to the world.

Instead, you must live out the rest of your life on this dreadful little rock,

knowing that your own *foolishness* has helped bring misery or death to every person you've ever cared for.

I'm not worthless. Or powerless!

357

Even if she didn't seem to believe you, she knows that you believe it, and she may yet act on it.

She could punish us all and have you as a prize. You won't be safe here any longer.

But you still have the proof. The letter from the king. She can't prove anything without that!

It is the only piece of proof that I possess. That does not mean that others do not exist, back in Albion.

Do you think that if Queen Catherine heard about you, she could not find them if she searched?

It isn't the letter that has made you safe, Margaret;

it is the fact that you yourself were a forgotten secret.

What are we going to do?

Captain Marley has a notion.

Bear in mind, I have not told him your secret— what he offers will put him in enough danger already.

Come in, Captain!

Mistress Margaret. It's because of the Elysian sisters, and Lady Cameron, that my Richard is alive and well.

He's standing outside the door now, keeping watch for us.

The Regina Maris can take you, and your lord and lady as well, away from the Island.

We'll put in at a quiet trading port, then arrange passage for you on a ship bound for the Continent.

But how will we get to the *Regina Maris* when Eleanor and Francis are locked in their rooms and guarded?

Won't Mother Mary Clemence know you've taken us? You'll be sent to prison, too!

I can take care of myself and my own men, Margaret.

We have keys to the chambers. We need only pick the right time to use them.

I have an idea.

It would make it seem as if we're not on the *Regina Maris* at all.

And it would give Queen Catherine a reason to be very angry with Mother Mary Clemence.

So angry that she might be sent to prison instead of any of *you*.

And how would we do that, Margaret?

You need to lock me in here for a few more hours.

Then you need to hide the coracle and tell Tess to add a special ingredient to tonight's bread.

Meet me here an hour before high tide.

I didn't like my own plan very much.

It was better than the one Sister Agnes and Captain Marley had, where everybody we left behind would suffer even more for saving Eleanor, Francis, and me. I spent the next few hours praying to Saint Elysia and Our Lady and the Sorrowful Son and God and everybody in between. I asked the Old People of the Island for their help, because we would need it, and I asked the Queen of the Sea to look out for us, too.

Please let this work.

No bells rang for None, so I wasn't certain what time it was when Sister Agnes knocked on the door again.

Mother Mary Clemence hadn't paid me another visit.

Margaret.

Where is Her Reverence?

Writing letters in my study. Carpenter and Yarrow are guarding the chambers.

We walked through the silent dorter—the sisters were all taking their midday rest, or pretending to.

Tess met us just outside the door to the Guest House.

Peter agreed to your plan straightaway. It's very clever!

I worried he might say no.

Pish! He knows that he must do everything his future bride asks of him!

Here is what we did.

Sister Agnes gave Tess the keys to the chambers in the Guest House where Francis and Eleanor were each being kept.

Then Tess baked those keys straight into Peter Yarrow's bread and delivered it on his supper plate.

Peter Yarrow was sitting in front of Francis's door at the far end of the hall, and Harold Carpenter was guarding Eleanor's chamber at the other end, near the stairway and the necessarium.

Once an hour, Harold Carpenter got up to stretch his legs and use the necessarium.

That's when Peter Yarrow unlocked Francis's door and let him out.

Peter locked the door behind him. Then they unlocked Eleanor's door and sent Francis inside.

Then Peter Yarrow returned to his seat,

just in time for Harold Carpenter to come back and sit down in front of Eleanor's chamber,

which looked just as closed and locked as it had when he had left.

Peter Yarrow pretended to fall asleep,

ZzzZzZzZzzZzZ

then pretended to
wake up from a dream

and called Harold
Carpenter over.

I thought
I heard voices
from inside.

It's still locked.
He can't get out.
You were just
dreaming.

But I'm
sure I heard
something!

Do you want to
wake Her Reverence
and say you need
the key, because you
had a nightmare?

But
what if...

While they argued,

Eleanor and Francis opened her chamber door and left, closing it softly and locking it behind them.

It would seem as if they truly had vanished—either by fairy magic or a holy miracle. After all, the keys were in a ring around Her Reverence's own belt buckle. And it would seem that there was never a time when both Francis and Eleanor could have been let out of their chambers and escaped down the staircase without being seen.

Next, we had to leave the convent.

You hid the coracle?

Yes, Margaret.

Now, don't let me see where you've gone.

Or any of the places on the Island. I had loved the thought of seeing some of the rest of the world. I hadn't thought about whether I would still want to see the rest of the world if it meant never coming home again.

The three of us sat in the cave together for the whole day that came. The sunlight that came through the spaces between the rocks above was thin and gray. When the tide came in and filled the tunnel, the sound of the waves and the echoes they made in the cave made it too loud to talk.

How long will we wait here?

Well,

Her Reverence has to notice that we've gone.

Then she'll probably start by searching the convent,

and then the rest of the top part of the Island.

When she finally comes down to the beach and sees that the coracle is missing,

If Sister Agnes rings the bell for Lauds, it means Mother Mary Clemence has stopped searching, and we can leave the cave as soon as the tide is low enough.

And if the bell doesn't ring?

Then... I don't know.

We waited until well after dark.

Are you sure it can be heard?

I heard every bell when I was here before.

That night, Francis and Eleanor stayed awake, talking. They thought I was asleep, and at least some of the time I was. It was good to hear their voices, mixing with the sound of the waves far down the beach.

I imagined that they were my mother and father,
and that I was still a small child, and they were
speaking softly to each other as I slept...

When I awoke,

Eleanor was not in the cave.

Where is...

She went outside for a moment. To...use the latrine.

You can sleep a bit longer, if you like. I'll wake you when I hear the bell.

No. I'm too nervous.

I heard a story this evening, Margaret.

It sounded like one of Jess's fairy tales, but it seems that this one is true.

378

The water felt colder than ever,

and the beach that met us
was dark and empty and gray.

The Regina Maris was
still visible in the bay.

It hadn't left us.

And Sister Agnes
was waiting.

386

I set aside one piece of clothing from each of us.

Then we tied up rocks in the rest.

Francis threw the weighted garments down into the water.

What will you do with the rest, Margaret?

We'll throw them into the water, too.

But throw them to the side, so they'll wash up on the beach.

Last of all, Francis kicked a hole into the coracle, and we pushed it out onto the water, to sink or to be broken up by the waves.

I hoped it wouldn't be too hard for the sisters to make a new one.

The clothes and the ruined boat, if they wash up on the beach...

everyone will think we've drowned.

I know.

I'm still no expert at swimming, though. Shall I tether a seal, or just ride on the fish like Saint Elysia?

Margaret and I can swim on either side of you.

Put your arms across our necks and we'll pull you along.

389

I'm not finished.

You have to pardon William, too, and his family.

You have to give everyone back their home and land that was taken away when they went to prison.

You want me to free an entire clan of warriors who swore to put an end to the very kingdom of Albion?

They didn't. They only wanted their own freedom.

You have to pardon them. All of them.

Or else I'm not coming with you.

For a long moment, I thought that I might have made a terrible mistake. That I would stand on that rock and watch Francis and Eleanor swim into the waves and drown, or reach the ship and sail away forever.

And what would become of me? I'd have to borrow a seal's skin and become a selkie and live among the waves. I would swim until the day I finally found the Queen of the Sea in her pale skin and Saint Elysia in her coracle. Together we would set out across the Silver Sea, for the peace and safety of whatever lay on the other side.

Of course, there is much more that I could
tell you about what happened next to the true
Queen of Albion and her companions.

But for now—

it is enough.